~ The Classic Tale of ~
Pigling Bland

D0604516

Based on the original story by Beatrix Potter with all new illustrations

Manufactured in U.S.A.

8 7 6 5 4 3 2 1

ISBN 1-56173-592-2

Cover illustration by Anita Nelson

Book illustrations by Sam Thiewes

Adapted by: Sylvia Root Tester

Publications International, Ltd.

Once upon a time there was an old pig named Aunt Pettitoes. She had four little girl pigs, named Cross-Patch, Wee-One, Yock-Yock, and Spot. And she had four little boy pigs, named Alexander, Pigling Bland, Chin-Chin, and Stumpy.

One day, Aunt Pettitoes said, "It is time for all of you to make your way in the world." So all her piglets, except Pigling Bland, rode away in a cart.

"Now, Pigling Bland, take these work papers to market so someone will hire you. Stay away from traps, hen roosts, and bacon and eggs. Remember to always walk upon your back legs." Aunt Pettitoes gave him a little lunch and eight peppermint candies. Then she waved him on his way.

Pigling Bland trotted down the road. To pass the time, he sang,

> "This little pig went to market,
> This little pig stayed home,
> This little pig had roast beef . . . ."

The song made Pigling Bland hungry. So he sat down and ate his lunch—every bit. He ate two of his eight peppermints, too. After his rest, Pigling Bland walked a little farther. He came to a sign that read: To Market, 5 miles; Over the Hills, 4 miles.

Pigling Bland thought he would never get to market before dark. He decided to take the shorter way over the hills. He walked and walked. It began to grow dark outside. The wind whistled and the trees creaked and groaned. He took several wrong turns, and was soon quite lost. He was frightened and cried, "Wee, wee, wee! I can't find my way home!"

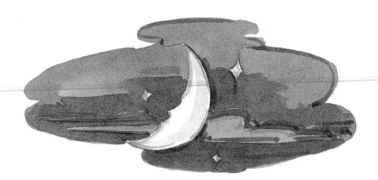

After much wandering, Pigling Bland saw a hen house. He hurried inside. "What else can I do?" asked Pigling.

"Bacon and eggs!" clucked a hen.

"Trap, trap, trap!" warned a rooster.

"To market, to market, jiggetty jig!" clucked another hen.

Just then, a man came to catch six chickens to take to market. His name was Mr. Piperson. He caught a white hen. Then he saw Pigling Bland squeezed up in a corner.

"What is this?" he exclaimed. "A pig! Just right for bacon and eggs!" He grabbed Pigling Bland and dropped him into a cage. Then he dropped in five more smelly, cackling hens.

Pigling Bland was nearly scratched to pieces.

At last Pigling Bland was lifted out of the cage. "What a find!" said Mr. Piperson. "You can sleep on the rug in front of the fire."

In the morning, Mr. Piperson made oatmeal. He poured it into three bowls. One was for himself, one was for Pigling Bland, and one was for . . . ?

Mr. Piperson glared at Pigling, so Pigling looked away. Mr. Piperson opened a closet door and walked in. He came out without the third bowl of oatmeal. He gobbled down his own breakfast and left for market with the six hens.

Pigling went on tiptoe to the locked door. He sniffed at the keyhole. All was quiet. Pigling pushed a peppermint under the door. It disappeared immediately! Pigling pushed the rest of his peppermints under the door.

When Mr. Piperson returned that night, he made more oatmeal. Again he took a bowl into the closet. But he didn't shut the door carefully; when he locked it, it didn't really lock. Then Mr. Piperson went to bed.

Pigling Bland sat by the fire and ate his supper. All at once, a little voice said, "My name is Pig-Wig. Make me more oatmeal, please!"

Pigling Bland nearly jumped out of his skin! A lovely little black pig stood smiling beside him. She pointed to Pigling's bowl. He quickly gave it to her. "How did you get here?" he asked.

"I was stolen for bacon and hams," replied Pig-Wig, with her mouth full.

"Stolen!" exclaimed Pigling Bland. "Oh, how terrible. Why don't you run away?"

"I will after supper," replied Pig-Wig. After she finished her second bowl of oatmeal, Pig-Wig got up to leave.

"You can't go in the dark," said Pigling Bland, "but if you wait until morning, I shall help you run away."

They agreed to wait until they could see the first light of day. With that taken care of, Pig-Wig settled in for a good night's sleep. Poor Pigling Bland was nervous. He stayed awake the whole night sitting in front of the fire. He sat there listening to make sure he could hear the snores Mr. Piperson made while sleeping.

They left early the next morning. The sun rose, and from the top of a hill they saw a bridge. They knew they'd be safe once they crossed it. Pigling stopped; he heard a noise. A grocer was coming along in his wagon.

"Leave the talking to me," whispered Pigling. "We may have to make a run for it." He pretended to be hurt and held Pig-Wig's arm.

"Two little pigs! Just right for bacon!" said the grocer. "Do you have working papers?" Pigling handed up his papers.

"These take care of you," said the grocer, "but they do not say anything about the girl pig." He saw a farmer plowing a nearby field. "Maybe she belongs to that farmer," the grocer said. "Wait here while I go ask him." The grocer drove off. A hurt pig could not run away.

"Now, Pig-Wig! Run NOW!" cried Pigling Bland.

Never did two pigs run as fast as these pigs ran! They raced and squealed and pelted down the hill toward the bridge. Pig-Wig's petticoats fluttered, and her feet went *pitter, patter, pitter.* They ran, ran, ran down the hill!

They came to the river,
    They came to the bridge,
They crossed it hand in hand—
    Then over the hills and far away . . .
Pig-Wig danced with Pigling Bland!